Helloooooo!

My name's **Ty**, and I'm seven, and I like **TONS** of things, but especially making stuff out of duct tape and drawing cartoon characters and being crazy. *Nice* crazy, though, like stuffing my knees in my shirt and jumping around—**BOING!**

I'm in this book, ONLY NOT REALLY BECAUSE THEN I'D BE VERY FLAT! But it is the story of me, and I hope you love it! ☺

THE LIFE OF TY

OF

PENGUIN PROBLEMS

THE LIFE OF TY

Penguin Problems

LAUREN MYRACLE

Illustrated by Jed Henry

PUFFIN BOOKS

An imprint of Penguin Group (USA)

PUFFIN BOOKS
Published by the Penguin Group
Penguin Group (USA) LLC
375 Hudson Street
New York, New York 10014

USA * Canada * UK * Ireland * Australia
New Zealand * India * South Africa * China

penguin.com
A Penguin Random House Company

First published in the United States of America by Dutton Children's Books,
a division of Penguin Young Readers Group, 2013
Published by Puffin Books, an imprint of Penguin Young Readers Group, 2014

THE LIBRARY OF CONGRESS HAS CATALOGED THE DUTTON EDITION AS FOLLOWS:
Myracle, Lauren, date.
The life of Ty : penguin problems / Lauren Myracle ; [illustrated by Jed Henry]. —First edition.
p. cm.
Summary: "Seven-year-old Ty gets into mischief and big-hearted schemes while navigating
second grade and becoming a big brother"—Provided by publisher.
ISBN 978-0-525-42264-8 (hardcover)
[1. Brothers and sisters—Fiction. 2. Schools—Fiction.] I. Henry, Jed, illustrator. II Title.
III. Title: Penguin problems.
PZ7.M9955Li 2013
[Fic]—dc23   2012045145

Puffin Books ISBN 978-0-14-242317-2

Printed in the United States of America

Designed by Irene Vandervoort

1 3 5 7 9 10 8 6 4 2

To Jamie and Jacob, two cool dudes. ☺

THE LIFE OF TY

PENGUIN PROBLEMS

CHAPTER ONE

Today, my big sister Sandra is taking me to school. She pulls into the drop-off lane and tells me to walk in by myself. She says, "Ty, you're seven years old. You can do this."

"I know," I say, because of course I can. I can do tons of things. When a spider needs rescuing in our house, I'm the one who does it. At school, on the playground, I'm famous for jumping from one wobbly mushroom thing to the next without falling. Also, I'm excellent at growing head-hair, which is good because it means I'm not bald.

I'm just not ready to go in *this very second*. It's more fun to sit in the car and watch for a while. Linnea's mom follows Linnea with a bakery box, which means it's probably Linnea's birthday and she's going to give out cupcakes. My book partner, Price, runs ahead of his mom and tugs on the heavy glass door. Only he's a preschooler, so his mom has to sneakily reach up high and help him.

My other sister, Winnie, twists around in the front seat. She's younger than Sandra, but older than me. "You like school," she reminds me. "You'll get to see Lexie. You'll get to be Bad Scary Dry Cleaners together."

"No, because Bad Scary Dry Cleaners ended a long time ago," I say.

Now Lexie and I are Boingees, which means we put our arms in our shirts and squat and hop all over the playground—*boingee boingee boingee!* Lexie's friend Breezie is *sometimes* a Boingee, only hardly ever.

Breezie doesn't like me. Winnie says Breezie wants Lexie all to herself.

Sandra honks. I jump.

"Ty. Out," she says. "*Now.*" She reaches back and opens my door. She shoves it so it swings open wider. Next, she shoves *me*. ON MY BOTTOM.

"Sandra!" I cry. I scurry out, but stick my head back in to say, "Sandra, you are so mean!"

"Bye," she says, pulling away from the curb.

My heart races. She's not supposed to pull away, *zoom,* without any warning.

"Fine! Bye!" I say. "And you're not mean. Not all the time. And, Winnie?" I blow a sneaky kiss, which boys *are* allowed to do.

"Catch it!" I call. "Did you catch it?"

Winnie leans out her window and grabs it out of the air. She pops it into her mouth. *"Mmm, butterscotch."*

She kisses her fingers and blows her kiss to me.

I catch, swallow, and say, "Ew! Dried mouse droppings!"

Winnie laughs. Her hair whips into her face as Sandra pulls away, and then . . . they're gone.

Now I *have* to go inside. My stomach tightens. Not because I'm nervous, because being nervous is babyish. Being nervous is for first graders or kindergartners.

But it used to be that Mom took me to school. She walked me all the way to my classroom, and we did our good-byes there.

Then Teensy Baby Maggie came along.

Then Sandra started driving me to school. For three whole weeks, she's driven me to school instead of Mom. At first, she did walk me in. Either she would or Winnie would.

Then today came along, and *bam*. Instead of walking me in, Sandra shoved me on my bottom, and Winnie let her.

Price's mother comes out of the building, this time without Price. I don't think she knows I'm Price's book partner, but she smiles at me anyway. I give her a small smile back. She heads to her car, and I bet she's thinking, *Why is that boy just standing there?*

Probably lots of people are thinking that. All the kids going in, all the parents coming out. I could stand here forever, but I'd get all wrinkly, and everyone would say, "Who's that old creepy dude who's always standing there?"

I start toward the door. Then I stop, because I hear a noise coming from the playground. A kid noise. Only kids aren't supposed to be on the playground yet. I go to check it out. It's Price. He's saying "Help!" in a squinchy voice, and the reason why is because his head is stuck between two metal bars.

I sigh.

Preschoolers.

I go through the gate outside the playground, and it clangs when I pull it shut. Price tries to look over, but he can't, really.

"Hold on, Price!" I call. "I'm coming!"

"My head got stuck!" he cries.

"I know!"

There are steps leading from the slides to the monkey bars, and by the stairs, there are rails that have metal bars. That's where Price is stuck. It's not the first time.

I walk over, bend at the waist, and put my upside-down face where he can see me.

"Ty!" he says happily. He tries to stand, but it doesn't work. *"Ouch."*

Boy, I'm glad I'm not a preschooler anymore.

"Have you drawn any more pictures of Cyber Grape?" Price asks.

Cyber Grape is like Plankton from SpongeBob, only bigger and purple, and I invented him. I drew a picture of him for Price, and now Price wants more and more.

I also invented Robo-Thing, who is Cyber Grape's best friend, but without as many superpowers.

Price doesn't know about Robo-Thing.

"I haven't drawn any Cyber Grape pictures this morning, because this morning I'm rescuing you," I say.

"Will you draw some more soon?"

"Maybe. Now, stay."

I tromp up the stairs. I tromp to the railing and kneel beside him. I reach through the bars, grab his head, and twist twist twist, until *pop!*

He topples backward and lands on the seat

of his jeans, which are the kind with elastic. He presses on his skull like he's pushing his brain into place. He looks at me with admiration. Like how Robo-Thing looks at Cyber Grape, probably. Huh. I haven't drawn that picture yet, but I should.

"Don't stick your head in there again," I tell Price. "And even so, you're not supposed to be out here. You're supposed to be inside."

I hold out my hand. His hand is sweaty, but I pull him up anyway. "C'mon. I'll walk you to your class."

CHAPTER TWO

By the time I get to Mrs. Webber's room, which is *my* class, I feel less stomach-jumpy than when I first got to school. I feel more like me. Even so, my hand gives Mrs. Webber a weird wave when I walk through the door. It does this without my permission, because I don't know the rule for saying hi to Mrs. Webber first thing in the morning.

Maybe there's not a rule?

"Good morning, Ty," Mrs. Webber says. "How's your baby sister doing?"

She always asks this. Every day for the last three weeks, she's asked this.

"She's fine," I tell her, which is what I always say. I think for a moment. "She spit up all over my mom's shirt this morning."

"Oh dear. No fun."

"Nope."

Mrs. Webber clucks. Then she says the other thing she always says, which is, "Well, be sure to help out your mom as much as you can. Babies are precious, but *so* much work."

"Babies aren't precious," Lexie says, coming up next to me. "Babies are b-o-r-i-n-g *boring*. Does she have hair yet?"

"Nope," I say. "Still bald."

"Ha. Ugly baldie." She grabs my arm. "Come on, let's go."

I follow her to the beanbag corner of the room. *Teensy Baby Maggie isn't ugly,* I almost tell her as we sit down. But I don't, and I also don't tell her that she shouldn't make fun of bald people in general, which she pretty much is by saying "baldie."

Joseph, who's my real best friend, is a baldie. A *temporary* baldie, because he has leukemia. He's going to be okay. But he's in the hospital for a little while. Not *forever*, just for a while.

But telling Lexie not to do something just makes her do it more, except when I'm trying on purpose to trick her. Then she doesn't fall for it. Like, if I say, "Don't give me your cheese puffs or I will be so mad," she shrugs and says, "Okay." And doesn't give me her cheese puffs.

Also, Lexie herself has really pretty hair. It's dark brown and shiny, and it swishes.

She bumps me with her shoulder and says, "Look what I learned to do. It's awesome."

She wiggles a rubber band off her wrist. She's wearing zillions of them. She holds the rubber band in one hand, and with her other hand, she makes a gun shape.

"Lexie?" I say.

She loops the rubber band around her thumb and the tip of the pointed finger. The rubber band slips off, but she gets it back on. Then, with her other hand, she pulls down the bottom of the rubber band, stretches it tight, and uses the leftover fingers on her gun hand to lock it in place.

My stomach knots up like it did at morning drop-off. "Lexie . . ."

She lets go, and the rubber band sails off her finger and thwacks the wall.

"Sweet!" she says. "Wasn't that sweet? Tomorrow, you need to bring lots of rubber bands so we can have a war, 'kay?"

She pulls another rubber band off her wrist. This time she aims it at Taylor—a boy Taylor—but before she can do anything, Mrs. Webber rings her cowbell and calls, "Room break!"

My muscles relax. I like saving people. I don't like shooting them.

Some of the kids in our class don't like Lexie because she's wild. Like, sometimes she kicks them or pokes them with sharp pencils. Sometimes, she kicks and pokes *me*. Sometimes I have to use my stern voice and say, "Lexie, stop."

But Lexie is big and loud. She does whatever she wants.

Sometimes—not *all* the time, but *some*times—I wonder if I   should be wild. Or at least a little wild. Or at least a little . . . something that's more wild and less stomach-clenchy.

Right now, I'm glad it's time for morning meeting.

"All right, kids," Mrs. Webber says once we're sitting crisscross applesauce on the floor in front of her. Taylor isn't allowed to sit next to Chase, but I can sit next to anybody, so I sit next to Lexie. Breezie sits next to Lexie, too. On Lexie's other side.

I *would* sit next to Joseph, but yeah . . . Joseph's in the hospital. I on purpose don't sit next to Taylor, because he's even wilder than Lexie, and he gets in trouble all the time. Also, he always wants to do puny-arm fights.

"On Thursday, we have our field trip to the Georgia Aquarium," Mrs. Webber says.

Everyone claps and says, "Yay!"

I can't wait to go to the aquarium. We'll get to touch sharks and real live starfish and see two beluga whales who are friends and who drift like pale gigantoid marshmallows through the water. Mrs. Webber told us about them. That's how I know.

"Please bring in your permission slip if you haven't already," Mrs. Webber says. "And a sack lunch, so we can throw our trash away when we're done."

Lexie raises her hand. "Can we bring money for the gift shop?"

"You cannot bring money for the gift shop.

That would be too complicated with the whole grade there."

"*Wah*," Lexie says.

Taylor raises his hand.

"Yes, Taylor?" Mrs. Webber says.

"I have a question," Taylor says.

"Does your question have to do with our field trip?"

"Yes."

"Then go ahead. But stay on topic."

"Well, it's just that the only black shirt I have is ripped, and so I can't wear it, and so I can't dress up as my favorite fish, the black phantom."

"Taylor? Did I at any point say that you should dress up as your favorite fish for our field trip?"

"I had a black phantom once in my aquarium. Then I got a kissing fish, and the kissing fish ate it."

Everyone laughs.

"Taylor . . ." Mrs. Webber starts.

"The kissing fish kissed it to death!" Lexie says.

"It happened on vacation," Taylor says. "I forgot to put food in the fish tank, and—"

"*Taylor.*"

"—and when we came back, the kissing fish was still there. But the black phantom was just a skeleton!"

"Ewww!" the girls say.

"Cool!" the boys say.

I think it's ewww *and* cool. I feel bad for the dead black phantom, though.

"Just a fishy fish skeleton, floating in the water," Taylor says.

"Taylor, you're off topic," Mrs. Webber says. "Now on Thursday, I'm going to put you into groups with parent volunteers, so—"

"But *can* we dress up as our favorite fish?" Taylor asks. "If we want to?"

"*No.*" Mrs. Webber looks hard at Taylor. Then smiles at the rest of us. Or tries to. "So if any of you have a preference for whose group you're in, let me know. I can't guarantee anything, but I'll do my best."

Taylor's hand shoots up.

"Let me know in private," Mrs. Webber says.

"But—"

"Moving on," Mrs. Webber says. "Can someone repeat back to me what you need to do before Thursday?"

I can. I put up my hand.

"Yes, Ty?"

"Bring our permission slip," I say. "Bring a Lunchable."

"It doesn't have to be a Lunchable. But yes, you need to be able to throw your trash away afterward, so no Tupperware containers or thermoses or lunch boxes."

I'm going to tell Mom it has to be a Lunchable, because I like Lunchables. Especially the Nachos Supreme with a Capri Sun.

"And . . . ?" Mrs. Webber says.

"Oh!" I say. "And if we want to be in someone's group, tell you."

"Beautiful, Ty. Excellent listening."

I feel warm. I fold my lips over to hide my smile.

"Tell Mrs. Webber to put you with Breezie's mom," Lexie says. "So we can be in the same group."

"Breezie's mom?"

"Unless your mom's chaperoning. Is she?"

Maybe she could. I didn't ask her. Or maybe I did, and she said no. But if I ask again, maybe she'll say yes.

Before Teensy Baby Maggie, Mom used to chaperone all the time. She went with us to the Atlanta Zoo and bought everyone in our group popcorn, which we shared with the howler monkeys.

"All right, morning meeting's over," Mrs. Webber says. "Head to your desks and get started on your reading work sessions."

Kids untangle their legs and push their hands against the carpet as they stand up. I get up, too, but *without* hands. I can do that, even from crisscross applesauce. I practiced and practiced, and now it's easy.

No one notices, but I don't care. Some things I'm good at just for me.

CHAPTER THREE

Sandra has track after school and Winnie is off with her friends, so I get Mom all to myself. She's pretty and she smells good, and we snuggle on the sofa and watch *Tom and Jerry*, just the two of us.

Teensy Baby Maggie is taking her nap.

"So how was your day, Ty-bug?" Mom asks. We can talk and watch the cartoon, because Tom and Jerry never say anything. There's just music as Jerry runs around inside the piano.

"Good," I say. "And we're going to the Georgia Aquarium on Thursday. I'm supposed to bring a Lunchable. Also, Mrs. Webber needs more chaperones. Can you be one? Please?"

"Sweetie . . ."

I frown. I hate that "sweetie," that sad sweetie

that says *you know I can't, and I'm sorry, but also you shouldn't have even asked, because now I have to use my sad sweetie voice.*

"You could bring Teensy Baby Maggie. She could be in her stroller."

"Mrs. Webber doesn't allow siblings. You know that."

"Then put her in her sling. You could say the sling was your purse."

Mom laughs. I don't want her to laugh. I want her to say, "What a good idea!"

"Anyway, she's not even a sibling. Not really." Because she's so teensy is why. "*Sss*oon she'll be a *sss*ibling, but right now she's just a *sss*. A *suh!*"

Mom roughs up my hair with her knuckles. "Sorry, bub. But you know what? You'll have a great time anyway."

"I know," I say. But I might or I might not. *I* get to choose. "I'll probably be put in Breezie's mom's group."

"Well, that's good."

"No."

"Will Lexie be with you and Breezie?"

"Maybe."

"Then *that's* good, isn't it?"

I think about Lexie's rubber-band gun. During math, when we were doing take-aways, Lexie shot a kitten. Not a real kitten, a kitten on a poster. The kitten was clinging to a tree. HANG IN THERE! it said underneath.

If the kitten had been real, it would have fallen. Instead of *five take away three*, Lexie would have taken away that kitten.

I think more about Lexie, like how she didn't eat her healthy crackers at snack time. She said they were gross. So I told her about Teensy Baby Maggie's gross crackers, which are called "teething biscuits" even though they're not biscuits and even though Maggie doesn't have a single tooth. And even though Teensy Baby

Maggie can't even eat them yet! A lady gave them to Mom at her baby shower, and now they're just sitting in our pantry. I tried one for the fun of it, only it wasn't fun.

"Why are they called teething biscuits if they're not for people with teeth?" Lexie said. "That's dumb."

Then she crushed one of her gross crackers to smithereens and said, "I don't want a baby sister, ever. If I saw someone without teeth, I would run and scream. And why do you have to call her Teensy Baby Maggie every single day of your life?"

"I don't have to. I just do." I pulled my eyebrows together. "Everyone does."

"Well, I think it's stupid," she said. She scattered her gross cracker crumbs on my shoe. "Were you Teensy Baby Ty when you were a baby? Or were you Stupid Baby Ty?"

I decide to stop thinking about Lexie.

"It's only half-good that I'll be in her group," I tell Mom. "Sometimes Lexie is annoying."

"Ah," Mom says. "And that is why it's all-the-way good that I got *you* as my son. I'm glad you're my Tyster."

"And I'm glad you're my Momster."

"A monster? You think I'm a *monster*?!"

I giggle.

She tickles me, and I giggle more.

"I can't believe you just called me a monster!" she says. "My own dearest, darlingest son!"

"*Momster*! Not *monster*!"

From the baby monitor on the kitchen counter, I hear a noise.

A bad noise. A worse-than-the-noise-Price-made-on-the-playground noise.

"Did you hear that?" Mom says.

I grab the remote and turn up the volume on the TV. "I love this part. The piano lid is going to slam down on Tom's head, see?"

"Ty, put that on mute, would you? I think I heard Baby Maggie."

If I had an extendable arm, I'd reach over to the baby monitor and put *it* on mute.

Mom tries to rise. I cling to her like a howler monkey.

"Ty, please."

She attempts to pry me off her. I don't let her. Every time she unlocks one part of me, I lock on with another. It's funny.

"When you were a baby, I went to you when you cried," she says. She stands up, and I slide down her body so that I'm wrapped around her leg.

"Ty, stop. It's *not* funny."

I let go. My cheeks get hot.

On the TV, the piano lid flattens Tom, and his paws and whiskers and tail stick out like a pancake. Mom is missing the good part, and she doesn't even care.

"I'll bring Maggie down here," Mom says. "I'll keep watching Bugs Bunny while I feed her."

It's not Bugs Bunny. It's Tom and Jerry! And Tom is so silly, and Jerry is so cute and little, and—

Never mind. Jerry's not cute, and I don't even like him. I *never* liked him. I grab the remote and turn off the TV.

From the baby monitor, I hear Mom get closer and closer to Teensy Baby Maggie's room. Then she's in there for real. I hear her say, "Hey there, Teense. How's my baby? How's my teensy bitsy Maggie-pie?"

Next come crinkle-sheet sounds, which mean Mom's lifting Maggie out of her crib. "Come on, bug. That's my good girl."

My chest goes up and down. *I'm* her bug. She's only supposed to call *me* "bug." And I don't like how Mom has to run run run to Maggie the very second she cries, either.

Also, Maggie's not as bitsy as everyone thinks. Spiders are bitsy, like the itsy-bitsy spider. Flies are bitsy. Jerry from *Tom and Jerry* is bitsy, but Maggie doesn't even know who Tom and Jerry are. She doesn't even know what cartoons are—and she made Mom miss the best piano-slamming part!

If someone made me miss the best part, I'd be mad and call that person a meanie-head.

So maybe Lexie's right. Maybe we shouldn't call Teensy Baby Maggie "Teensy Baby Maggie" anymore.

We should call her Big Fat Meanie Baby instead.

CHAPTER FOUR

When I wake up the next morning, there's something under my bed.

It's past seven o'clock, and Mom has told me three times to GET UP. But I can't, because the thing under my bed is bumping and lashing its tail. It's Winnie's cat, Sweetie-Pie. Every time I sneakily sneak my foot out, Sweetie-Pie swipes at it.

I hear Mom on the staircase. She's heading toward my room. *Uh-oh.*

"Ty, this is the third time I've had to call you to breakfast," she says, sagging against the door frame.

The fourth, actually. "I'm getting up. I promise."

"Baby, you're not. You're lying there like a lump."

"Okay, but . . ."

"No 'buts,'" she says, and she uses her sharp voice. "Get your hindquarters moving, bucko."

Then she just leaves! Without even asking what's making me stay stuck in bed!

I stick my tongue out at her even though she's gone. Teensy Baby Maggie gets to sleep in her crib, la la la, until Mom goes and gets her. *I* have to get up by myself, only I can't because of Sweetie-Pie.

I stick my tongue out at Teensy Baby Maggie, even though she's in her own room. In my head, I say, *Big Fat Meanie Baby*.

It cheers me up, so I say it outside my head. But quietly. "Poop on you, you Big Fat Meanie Baby!"

Anyway, cribs are stupid. They're like cages, and if Price came over and climbed into Maggie's crib? He'd get his head stuck between the bars for sure.

I imagine Price in Maggie's crib. I imagine his head sticking out between the wooden bars, and I giggle my man-giggle. My man-giggle is awesome. I use my stomach muscles to push it out—*heh heh heh*—and Winnie says it makes me sound like an evil criminal.

Then I remember that I still don't know how to get out of bed because of Sweetie-Pie, and being scared of a cat makes me feel like a scaredy-cat. It dries up all my man-giggles.

I'm not usually scared of Sweetie-Pie. When she sits in my lap, I pat her and say, "Good Sweetie-Pie." Then Winnie pats me and says, "Good Ty. Good Ty for petting my good cat."

Hey! That gives me an idea! Sweetie-Pie *is* Winnie's sometimes-good-sometimes-sneaky-clawed cat, so I use a whispery yell to call out, "Winnie!"

"What?" Winnie calls back.

"I need you!"

"Why?"

"I just do!"

She growls, loud enough for me to hear. But she comes to my room. "Yes?"

"Sweetie-Pie's under my bed."

"So?"

"If I put my foot out, she'll eat it."

"She will not."

"She might."

"Then stand up and *jump* off, so she can't reach you."

"What if she's in a pouncing mood?"

Winnie puts her hands on her hips. "Ty, you're acting babyish. Just get out of bed."

My ribs go *whooomph,* like someone tied a rope around them and pulled it tight.

"Never mind," I say. "You can leave now."

She does.

Sweetie-Pie meows.

◻ ◻ ◻

It's my pee that finally gets me. I hold it until I can't anymore. Until I almost explode, which would be awesome, but messy. Tinkle-sprinkles everywhere! *Ahhhh!*

I lean over my bed and say, "Sweetie-Pie, *out*."

Her eyes gleam. I jerk back.

What am I going to do?

There's no point calling for Sandra. She'd say, "Deal with it yourself. You're a big guy." And Dad's already left for work. So what do I *do*?

If I had a broom, I could jab her out.

If I had an eagle, the eagle could swoop down and grab her and fly off into the distance. Bye-bye, Sweetie-Pie!

Only that would be sad, because the eagle would eat her. Anyway, I don't have an eagle.

I *do* have eagle eyes, though. Mom's always telling me that. She'll say, "Ty, will you see if you can find the safety pin I dropped?" And when I do, she says, "You, my darling dude, have eagle eyes. Thank you."

I turn on my eagle eyes and scan my room. There's got to be *something* I can use.

My Lava lamp?

My copy of *Toys Go Out*?

How about . . . *ah-ha!* My old pal the Dustbuster! Mom gave it to me because I love it, and because I begged. I get lots of things that way:

—a gold belt of Winnie's with two hearts that hook together. I think it came from a pirate ship.

—a dragon puppet I gave Dad for Father's Day.

—one of Teensy Baby Maggie's burp cloths because it already *was* mine. It says TY on it and everything. So even though it was a handy-down, Mom wasn't allowed to say, "Here, Teensy Baby Maggie, this can be yours now." It has a football embroidered on it, and a little boy wearing a red cap and a yellow shirt, and it's *mine*.

The Dustbuster is blue and called "The Shark." It's cordless except when it's plugged into the wall. When the light on the side is red, the battery needs charging. When the light is green, Sharkie is ready to suck up anything in its way.

I kick off my covers and scooch to the end of my bed closest to my dresser. That's where Sharkie lives, plugged into an outlet in the wall.

His charged-up light is green. *Yes.*

I think for a bit, and then I wrap my hand in my sheet. I lean off my bed and *s-t-r-e-t-c-h* over the ocean of carpet, and I almost fall. But I don't! I grab Sharkie and sit back on my bed. I yank the cord out of its bottom, and when it falls to the ground, a black-and-white paw snakes out and snags it.

I think, *Too bad for you, Sweetie-Pie, because the cord is just a cord.* Sharkie, on the other hand, knows how to roar.

I aim Sharkie under the bed and slide the power button to ON. *ROOOOAAAAAAARRRRRRRR!!!!!!!*

Sweetie-Pie yowls and dashes out. Her fur goes spiky like Tom's from *Tom and Jerry,* and her ears pull back. I hop out of bed and chase her, jutting Sharkie in front of me.

"Hai-ya!" I cry. "Hai-ya, hai-ya!"

Mom yells something.

"What?" I yell back.

Sandra, from her bedroom, yells something.

"What???"

Winnie storms into my room. "Ty!" she says angrily. She snatches Sharkie out of my hand and switches off the power.

The roar dies down.

Now I hear what all the yelling was about, because . . . someone else is yelling, too. Someone who isn't Mom or Sandra. Except actually, the someone isn't yelling so much as making really high fire engine siren sounds.

I suck in a BIG *uh-oh* breath.

"Great, Ty," Winnie says. "You woke up Maggie. That's just great."

She spins around to go to get her and passes right by Sandra, who stomps into my room and glares. Sandra is pretty like a princess, but not right now.

"*God,* Ty," she says. "What is *wrong* with you?"

More stomping sounds come from the staircase. Double-triple uh-oh.

Mom sticks her head into my room. Her mouth is a Magic Marker slash. "Ty, I asked you to do one thing," she says in a voice even worse than her sharp voice. "I asked. You. *To please be quiet.*"

I take a step backward and almost stumble.

She doesn't care. She says, "And so you turned on the Dustbuster and screamed like a banshee?"

"I didn't—"

"Don't," she says, and *not* like a Momster. Like

a monster. "Just *go*, Ty. Go downstairs and fix yourself a bowl of Cheerios."

My blood does a weird thing in my head, like *bum bum bum*. Moms aren't supposed to say *just go*.

Winnie returns with Teensy Baby Maggie, who's wailing.

Mom takes her and holds her close and pats her back, and since looking at Mom is scary, I look at Teensy Baby Maggie's bald head. She's not bald everywhere. Just in one round spot.

Baby Maggie's un-bald hair is the color of the dishwashing stuff Mom keeps under the kitchen sink. Pale, pale, very pale gold.

My hair is the color of honey, Mom says, but really it's brown.

"I am going to try—*try*—to rock Maggie back to sleep," Mom says. "I got three hours of sleep last night, and if I don't get a nap, there's a good chance I'll have to check myself into a mental institution."

No one speaks.

"Sandra, can I count on you to get everyone to school on time?"

"Yeah. I mean, *yes*. Of course."

"All right. Fine. Then I'll see you all when you get home." She turns to go.

"Wait!" I say.

She turns back.

"Hug?" I say in a smallish way.

Mom doesn't want to. *She doesn't want to hug her own son.* I can see it on her face.

Stupid hot wet splots push their way into my eyes. Stupid, stupid, stupid.

Mom sighs. She shifts Teensy Baby Maggie to one arm and opens her other arm. I go to her, and she hugs me.

"Kiss?" I say in an even smallisher way.

She kisses my cheek. Then she says, "Now, go. All of you. I love you, but I'm beat."

Mom shuffles out of my room, and Teensy

Baby Maggie—Big Fat *Meanie* Baby!—gazes at me over Mom's shoulder. Her head bobs as Mom walks, and her eyes are wide, like she's surprised.

But I think she's faking.

I think she likes hogging Mom all to herself.

CHAPTER FIVE

At school, when it's time for recess, I have to play with Taylor because Lexie's grouchy at me. She's grouchy because I'm not wearing any rubber bands. I don't have any in my pockets, either.

"Did you forget?" Lexie demanded when she found out.

"I don't want to do rubber-band guns," I told her. "Let's do something else."

"I don't want to do something else."

"We could be Boingees," I said.

She made a sound like being Boingees was dumb, when she's the one who invented Boingees. Well, we both did. Then she went to find Breezie.

That's why I'm stuck with Taylor.

He says, "Let's do puny arms."

I say, "I don't want to do puny arms."

He says, "Then I'm going to put you in a headlock," and he will, because he has before. And if he puts me in a headlock, I'll have to kick him in the shin, and then I'll have to scramble up and *run*. Then I'll have no one to play with.

So, fine. We do puny arms. We draw our arms up into our sleeves so that our elbows are inside our shirts and the only parts sticking out are our hands.

We slap each other with them, and I laugh. Puny arms *can* be fun, which I forgot. Lexie is over by the fence with Breezie. Even so, I don't look at her. Well, sometimes I do.

"Now let's be robots!" Taylor says. "Robots in a robot war!" He lands a good one on my shoulder. *Thwack!*

"Okay, only let's be something else instead," I say. Because robots wouldn't have puny arms unless their maker made them wrong, and then they'd get thrown in the trash. We *could* be robots in a trash heap, but another idea pops into my mind.

"Let's be babies! Giant babies who can't even talk, and all they can do is go *waa waa waa* and flap their giant puny arms."

"Yeah!" Taylor says. He turns his body sideways and swats me. *"Waa! Waa!* I'm a big dumb baby!"

"Waa!" I say. I swat his hand with mine. "I'm a bigger, dumber baby! Better watch out, or I'll poop on you!"

Taylor scoots sideways. He keeps flapping. "If you poop on me, I'll poop on you. And pee. And stab you with a sword!"

"Yeah?" I say. "Well, I'll throw a *pacifier* at you! A yucky, gross, spitty one!"

Baby Maggie doesn't use pacifiers, but I did. Mom says I had a zillion different pacifiers when I was a baby, and I slept with all of them. She says I'd suck on one for thirty seconds, then spit it out and pop in another. *Suck, spit, pop. Suck, spit, pop.* I think it sounds very cute of me.

Then, when I turned three, Mom told me I had to give my pacifiers to a new child. That was THE LAW, she said, and I remember this part of the story myself. Only Mom didn't really give my pacifiers to a new child. She just put them in a cup on the shelf above the refrigerator. She admitted it after Teensy Baby Maggie was born.

Hmm. After school I'll ask her to get them down for me, so I can look at them.

Taylor flaps his puny arms. "Passies are for babies!"

"We *are* babies!" I remind him.

He lunges close and thwaps me *hard*. My head snaps back, and Taylor laughs.

"Taylor, *stop and I mean it!*" I say in a not-me voice. I think I taste blood, and inside of me is a big, hot, mad feeling, so maybe it's a mad voice. Super mad, because I don't like it when people laugh at me. Also, I might be getting teary again—for the second time this day!—and I really don't like people seeing my tears.

"*You're* a *big* dumb *bay*-bee!" Taylor chants. "*You're* a *big* dumb *bay*-bee!"

I could tell on Taylor. He'd have to run a lap around the playground. Instead, I walk away. Away from him. Away from everybody. I lean against the big gray trash bin and touch my tooth with my tongue.

It moves.

Taylor made my tooth loose. One of my *top* teeth, the one that's in the exact front. Except I have two front teeth, and Taylor whacked the one on the right, and now it wiggles.

"Ty?" Mrs. Webber says.

I jump. Where did *she* come from? I quickly

wipe my eyes, hoping I'm not tearstained.

"Are you hiding behind the trash can?" Mrs. Webber asks.

"What? No. I just like it here."

"Ah," Mrs. Webber says. "Well, can you please be Price's bathroom buddy?"

Price is standing next to Mrs. Webber. I didn't see him till now. He's holding the part of his pants where the zipper is, which I would never do. Which I never *did* do, even in preschool.

"Um, sure. Come on, Price."

Inside the school, Price walks fast, but with stiff zombie legs.

"It's a bad pee," he tells me.

I think of my morning pee, and I speed up my walking. We reach the boys' bathroom, and I say, "We made it! Yay!"

Price gazes at me.

I swing my hand at the urinals. "Go on. I won't watch."

Price keeps gazing at me. His eyes are round and not like Robo-Thing's eyes at all.

"Price? Don't you need to use the bathroom?"

His forehead gets scrunchy-worried, and I smell a smell. *Ohhhhh.*

"All right, um, don't worry," I say. "You stay here. I'll be right back." At the door, I glance over my shoulder. "Don't leave."

He sucks his lower lip and nods. *He'll* be tearstained soon if he's not careful.

I dash to the office and whisper in Ms. Betsill's ear. She is very nice and not mean at all and gives me a brown plastic grocery bag with spare pants and underwear in it.

"We ask parents to donate used clothing for just this sort of thing," she says.

Back in the boys' bathroom, I hand Price the bag.

He looks inside. "There's underwear in here."

"And pants. Yep."

"Bob the Builder underwear."

I peer into the bag. Sure enough, there's Bob in his yellow hard hat, driving around the underwear in a dump truck. A *dump* truck. Ha.

But Price is still worried, so I say, "I like Bob the Builder. And they're clean, so . . . yeah."

"But they're not mine."

"I know. They're loaners." I show him the waistband of the underwear. "They say TRINITY ELEMENTARY, see? You wear them now and bring them back tomorrow."

"Oh." Price shifts his weight. "What do I do with . . . um . . . ?"

That's a good question. What *is* he supposed to do with his own underwear and pants?

"I guess put them in the plastic bag? But go to the bathroom first."

He turns bright red. "I already did."

Which I already know, but I try to be nice like Ms. Betsill.

"Go into one of the stalls," I tell him, because

there are urinals *and* stalls in the boys' bathroom. "Take your pants and underwear off and put the new ones on. Then put yours in the bag. And then we need to get back to recess."

Price's face relaxes. "Okay," he says. "Okay, Ty."

Within the stall, he makes preschooler sounds—grunts and mouth-breathing and stuff—and I examine my tooth in the mirror.

"Done," Price says proudly. He holds out the plastic bag. After a second or two, I take it. We both wash our hands.

We go down the preschool hall, and I hang the bag on Price's hook. After that, we go back outside. Price runs off. Then he runs back and hugs me. Then he runs off again.

For the rest of recess, I mainly just stand there. Lexie and Breezie walk by, and Breezie tosses her hair. She links her arm through Lexie's and says, "Boys are so childish, don't you think?"

Lexie looks at the sky. "Sometimes yes, sometimes no."

I think about Price, who is a boy. Breezie would definitely call Price *childish*, if she knew what he did.

But guess what? I'd rather play with Price than Breezie any day. I don't want to play with Price or Breezie, but if I had to, I'd pick Price.

CHAPTER SIX

When I get home, I tell Mom about my loose tooth. She's supposed to say, "Oh my goodness!" and be shocked. Instead she says, "Yeah? That's great, Ty."

That's *great*? She is not listening. She's fixing dinner, and Baby Maggie is strapped to her like a caboose. I mean papoose.

"No, because it didn't get loose on its own," I say. "It's only loose because Taylor hit me."

"What?!" Mom swivels. Baby Maggie swivels with her. "*Who* hit you?"

"Taylor! Right in the mouth! I *told* you!"

She comes over to look, and she says, "Oh, sweetheart. My poor baby!"

I'm not a baby, because Maggie's the baby, and even so, I'm seven.

But I don't mind.

Just this once.

She hugs me, and in the middle of it, she sniffs my head. "Ty. You have *got* to take a bath."

"I think I'll pass, but thanks for the offer," I say politely. I'm not a fan of baths.

"Wrong answer, bug," Mom says. "You don't want to be the kid who everyone says, '*Ooo*, he smells' about."

"Yes, I do." Except I think about Price, and I know she's right.

"Bath. Tonight. Especially since you have a field trip tomorrow."

"The field trip isn't tomorrow. It's the day *after* tomorrow. Did you buy my Lunchable?"

"Not yet. I will. Now back to Taylor. Did you tell a teacher he hit you?"

I shrug.

"Maybe you should hang out with someone else during recess," she suggests.

Maybe, but who? Lexie was doing rubber-band guns. And it was fun being Big Fat Babies until Taylor whacked me.

I remember something, and my brain lights up.

"Hey, Mom? Can you get down my old pacifiers?"

"Your old . . . ? No, Ty. Why in the world do you want your old pacifiers?"

I eye the cabinet above the fridge. "Please?"

Teensy Baby Maggie *pluhs*. Mom groans. There's a dribbly bit of yuck on her shirt.

"Ty, I'm trying to fix dinner *and* take care of Maggie," she says. "I can't do everything."

"I just want to see them."

"Not now."

"When?"

"I don't know, Ty. When you can get them down for yourself. Why don't you go play on your Wii, okay?"

Because I don't want to play on my Wii. I want to see my old pacifiers. And since Mom said "when you can get them down for yourself," then I will.

Because I can.

I drag a stool over to the fridge.

"Ty, don't you climb on that," Mom warns, even though she's facing the sink. She thinks stools are only for sitting on, because they're high and the seat part is just a round circle. But I have very good balance. I *might* be a circus person one day.

But, fine. I'll climb on the counter. Mom doesn't think counters are for climbing on, either, but I *know* they are. Otherwise why would they be there?

I hear Dad pull into the driveway, which isn't the best news. Dad also doesn't think counters are for climbing on. But the good news is that the garage-door-opening noise will cover up my climbing sounds.

Vrrrrmmmmmm. The garage door rattles, and I backward bottom-hop onto the counter by the fridge. I twist around, get to my knees, and rise to my feet. So far, so good, even in my socks.

Clunk clunk clunk. That means the garage door is almost open, because that sound isn't supposed to happen. Dad keeps saying he needs to get it fixed.

With my left hand, I hold on to the cabinet closest to me. With my right hand, I reach for the cabinet above the fridge. My arm isn't long enough, so I stand on my tiptoes and use finger nudgings to coax it open. *Come on, cabinet door,* I tell it. *That's right. Just a little farther.*

It opens! On the shelf is a glass bottle filled with brown stuff, and next to that is the hot glue gun. Behind the hot glue gun is a six-pack of Perrier. Behind the Perrier is . . . *yes!* A plastic kids cup from the Olive Garden with pacifiers sticking out of it!

The garage door thunks to a stop. I hear Dad's car door open, I hear Dad's door shut. I hear the

garage door start to go down. All of this means
hurry.

I pretend I do have an extendable arm, and
I grope for the Olive Garden cup. I'm touching
it . . . I've almost got it . . . *come on, come on*—

The back door opens, and one second later—
half a second later—Dad's deep voice says, "*Ty.
Get off the counter.*"

I almost fall from being startled, but I catch
myself, and I don't give up on my mission. "Mom
said I could! Mom said if I could get them myself,
then I could!"

"Excuse me?" Mom says. Then, "Ty! What are
you *doing* up there?"

My finger wiggles over the rim of the cup.

"*Ty,*" Dad says, coming my way. "When I tell you
to do something, I expect you to do it." He *lifts*
me off the counter, and my scrambling fingers
tip over the Olive Garden cup. The cup and the
pacifiers clatter to the floor.

"Go to your room, Ty," Dad says. "You just earned yourself a break."

I kneel and gather the pacifiers. There are a lot of them, seven or eight, and they have cute pictures on them. A car. An elephant. A teddy bear.

"But, Dad . . ." I say.

"Keep arguing, and it'll be even longer."

I bundle the pacifiers in my shirt and go upstairs. Well, not all the way up, but far enough that they can't see me.

I don't like being sent to my room.

"Sorry, Joel," I hear Mom say. "I didn't know what he was doing. You have no idea how long a day it's been."

Dad lets out a big breath. "Well, I shouldn't have snapped at him. He scared me, that's all."

"It scared me, too. And just so you know, I did *not* give him permission to climb up there."

What? Yes, she did.

"He needs more attention," Mom says. "The baby . . . me being tired all the time . . ."

I get a tightness in my chest. I scooch one step farther up.

"Don't worry, Ellen. Ty is okay, and you're okay. We're all okay." There's a smooch sound. "But I'll go talk to him."

His footsteps come toward the stairs, and I scurry to my room. I shove my pacifiers under my pillow just in time. Phew!

Only, Dad passes right by. He said he was coming to talk to me, but he doesn't. He just passes right by.

Here is what I learn about pacifiers. I like them! When I suck one, it's like something safe is pressing up close.

Another interesting thing is their smell. They smell like my pillow, when I first wake up.

I hold the green teddy bear pacifier to my nose

and breathe in. Then, right at the very second when I've stopped expecting him, Dad appears out of nowhere. I shove the green pacifier under my leg. The others are by my crossed legs. I swoop them behind my back.

"Hey, bud," Dad says. "Can we talk, man to man?"

"Okay. How was your day?"

He settles himself on the edge of my bed. "Having a new baby in the house . . . It's a big change, huh?"

"No."

He studies me. He's got beard stubble on his chin.

"Are you doing okay with it?" he asks.

"What 'it'?"

"The new baby. Baby Maggie."

"Baby Maggie's an 'it'?"

Dad bows his head. He breathes. He looks back at me and says, "I know she takes up a lot of Mom's attention. And she cries sometimes. But she's kind of cute, don't you think?"

"Like seaweed," I mutter.

"*Seaweed?* How is your sister like seaweed?"

"The way her arms wave about. Like seaweed deep in the ocean."

"Ahhh. But your sister is a little girl."

My face warms up. I never said she wasn't.

We sit there. Finally, Dad smacks his hands against his thighs and pushes himself up. "Well, try to help your mother out. Don't cause her any trouble. And why don't you give me those pacifiers, huh? I think it's time we got rid of them."

"Why?"

"Because pacifiers are for babies. And you, Ty, are a big guy."

"I won't *use* them. I just want to *keep* them."

Dad holds out his hand. "C'mon, buddy. Pass 'em over."

My stomach tightens.

His hand stays where it is.

I scowl and give him the seven pacifiers that were behind my back. Greenie is a hard plastic lump beneath me. So? I don't look at Dad, because I don't even want to.

"Thank you," Dad says.

"Don't throw them away," I say. "I want to give them to my own children one day."

"Ty," Dad says wearily. "When you have kids, you can buy them new pacifiers. These are too old." He tugs on the rubber tip of the blue pacifier, *and part of it comes off*. What's left is a ragged hole.

Dad looks shocked. He stands up straighter and says, "See? If a baby was sucking on that, the baby would have choked."

I dig my fingernails into my palms. I would have *never* ripped off the head of my blue pacifier. Also, I want to touch the torn part. But I can't. Dad would say no.

Dad puts all the pacifiers into his pockets,

plus the scrap of rubber that used to be part of the blue one. The way he does it says, *There. Done.*

What he doesn't know is that I still have my green one.

CHAPTER SEVEN

fter school the next day, Sandra takes me to Piedmont Hospital to visit my best friend, Joseph. Piedmont Hospital is where Teensy Baby Maggie was born, so I know all about it; plus I've visited Joseph before. I even have permission to visit Joseph without having a parent with me. Sandra drops me off at the front entrance and says she'll be back in an hour.

I wave at the nurses in the Pediatric Ward. They wave back. When I get to room 512, I peek through the crack to see if Joseph's mom is in there, and when she isn't, I barge in and go, "Boo!"

Joseph jumps in his hospital bed and screams like a girl. Or a dolphin. They sound the same.

"Hi," I say, grinning.

Joseph grins back. "Hi. Do it again."

So I go, *"Boo,"* and he screams like a dolphin. We crack up.

And then we just talk. About gum-by-the-foot, about a mole on one of the nurse's cheeks, about alligators and how they let their meat rot before eating it. Joseph reads a lot, so he knows all kinds of stuff.

I tell him about Lexie, and how she was mad at me, but how she isn't anymore. He tells me his white blood cells are getting better, and I say, "That's awesome." I *really* want him to come back to school.

When it's time for me to leave, he says, "You stink, by the way. Like, smelly-stink."

I look down at myself. I sniff.

"It's okay, though," he says. "I don't care."

"I don't care, either," I say. I kind of do and kind of don't. "I was supposed to take a bath last night, but I didn't."

"Cool."

"I'm not going to take one tonight, either. I'm going for an Olympic record."

He gives me a thumbs-up and lies back against his pillow. "Cool."

I'm a man of my word and *don't* take a bath that night, just like I said. Mom tells me to right after supper, but I hop into bed instead, and then ka-boom! I wake up and it's Thursday, the day of our field trip! Sharks! Starfish! Beluga whales!

I wake up so excited, and then *whoosh,* my excitement gets sucked out of me, like someone sucked it out with a giant Dustbuster. Only not a fun Dustbuster.

First, I find out that Mom forgot to buy my Lunchable, and that I have to bring a juice box, an apple, chips, and a peanut butter and jelly sandwich in a stupid plastic grocery store bag. When I get mad, she says, "Ty, I hate to break it to you, but the world doesn't always revolve around you."

That makes me madder, and also hurts my feelings, because saying that is like saying I'm acting like a baby, when I'm not.

Then, at school, Lexie is back to being more friends with Breezie than with me. Breezie's mom, Mrs. Hammerdorfer, is our chaperone, and Lexie wants to show off by being Breezie's specialiest friend. That's what I think.

Even so, I try to win her back.

"Hammerdorfer," I whisper in her ear as Mrs. Webber has us line up by the door of our classroom. "*Hammer*dorfer."

She pretends not to hear.

"Someone should only have that name if they smash things with hammers," I whisper.

"Ty, hush," she says, without whispering. "It's not nice to make fun of people's names."

Mrs. Hammerdorfer pinches up her lips at me.

"'Hammerdorfer' is an old German name,"

Breezie says prissily. "The Hammerdorfers come from great wealth. Do you come from great wealth, Ty?"

I stomp on her toe, only not really. I *do* pretend she's a bug, and not the cute kind.

"Mmm-hmm," she says, like she knew it all along.

The third bad thing is that the sand shark exhibit isn't open, so we can't pet the sharks, and the fourth bad thing is that the beluga whales stay in their special private area and don't come out. I really wanted to see their giant, marshmallow bodies. I didn't know how much until now.

"Can we stop and eat lunch?" Lexie asks after she, Breezie, Breezie's mom, and I have walked around the aquarium for five thousand hours.

"I think that's a fine idea," Mrs. Hammerdorfer says.

There's an eating area in the middle of the aquarium, with puffy green sofas and chairs, and we plop down and pull out our lunches. Lexie has a Mini Hot Dogs Lunchable, and each mini hot dog has its own mini bun. Breezie has a Grilled Chicken Wrap Lunchable with a special Lunchables Brigade trading card. She gets Abel the Super Inventor, the rarest trading card there is.

I eat my peanut butter and jelly sandwich and don't even care.

Lexie whispers something to Breezie.

"Hey, Mom?" Breezie says. "Can we go to the gift store?"

My eyes fly to her, then to Lexie. Then to the gift store, which is across the way.

Breezie's mom glances at the other kids scattered around the food court area. Most of them are still eating. She glances at her watch and says, "I suppose."

I yelp.

"What's wrong, Ty?" Lexie says. Her eyebrows go up innocently, but there is a glint in her eyeballs that says, *You keep your mouth shut about Mrs. Webber and her stupid rules, mister.*

I breathe through my nose, loudly and quickly.

"You sound like a bull," Lexie says.

"Do not."

"A bull shark," Breezie says. "Also known as the Zambezi shark."

Her mother looks at her like she's a miracle. I look at her like she's a Zambezi bug, and not the cute kind.

"Anyway, are you coming?" Lexie asks.

"I haven't finished my chips."

She gets up. So does Breezie. "Okay, bye," they say, and they flounce off.

Mrs. Hammerdorfer pats her mouth with her napkin and folds her napkin into a small square. "I'm going to chat with Jordan's mom for a bit," she says, and *she* gets up and goes to another sofa with another mom on it.

So now it's just me and my Fritos and the crusts

of my sandwich. And a juice box. I'm not angry at the juice box, but I'm not *happy* at it, either.

I put a Frito in my mouth and chew chew chew while I watch Lexie and Breezie through the gift shop's glass window. There are breakable things in there like glass whales, which I would like to hold and which they *are* holding. If they break one, they could get in big trouble. Our whole class could get in big trouble!

Nobody likes a tattletale, but Mrs. Webber needs to know what Lexie and Breezie are doing. I'll just *mention* it, that's all. I shove my lunch trash into my backpack. I peek at Lexie and Breezie—yep, still in the gift shop—then go to Mrs. Webber's group.

"Excuse me, Mrs. Webber?"

"Hi, Ty," Mrs. Webber says. "Are you having fun?"

"Uh-huh. But I need to tell you something."

Hannah, Chase, and Taylor gaze at me. Taylor is always in Mrs. Webber's group because none of the parent chaperones want him.

"Yes?" Mrs. Webber says.

"Well," I start, "it's just that Lexie and Breezie went to the gift store, and you said not to, and . . . well . . . yeah."

"Oh dear," Mrs. Webber says. She sounds annoyed, but not *terribly* annoyed. She glances toward the gift store. So do Hannah, Chase, and Taylor. So do I.

"Lexie's about to do the claw game!" Taylor announces.

He's right. Lexie and Breezie are over by the game where zillions of stuffed sea creatures live in a big glass case. To play it, you put in two quarters and use a joystick to move a steel claw around. You have twenty seconds, and then *bam,* the claw drops down and closes. If it grabs on to something *and* carries it all the way to the chute, then the stuffed animal drops through the chute and you get to keep it.

"My dad never lets me do that game," Hannah says. "He says, 'You're just throwing your money away.'"

"I'm not allowed, either," Chase says. "Even with my own allowance."

"Because the claw never holds on to anything, even it if grabs it," I say. "Nobody *ever* wins. Right, Mrs. Webber?"

"Should I go stop her?" Hannah says. Hannah likes stopping people.

In the gift shop, Lexie digs around in her pocket. I want Mrs. Webber to hurry and tell Hannah, "Yes, go stop her and tell her she's in big trouble."

But Mrs. Webber smiles a funny smile. "You know what? Let's let the situation play out on its own."

"Huh?" Hannah says.

"You kids are right," she say. "Lexie and Breezie aren't supposed to be over there. When they lose their money, maybe they'll learn a lesson."

Will they lose their money AND get in trouble? I want to ask. I want Mrs. Webber to give them a lecture and make them take a time-out.

Lexie slides her quarters into the machine. The claw starts moving. Lexie leans forward, working the joystick.

"She has one! She has one!" Hannah squeals when the claw closes around a black-and-white dolphin. I see Breezie bring her fists to her mouth. I bet she's saying, "*Eeeee!*"

"She has *two*," Chase says in awe.

I squint. The claw, when it goes up, is clutching the black-and-white dolphin *and* a fuzzy blue dolphin. *Two* dolphins. Two dolphins in one claw.

"She still has to get them to the drop-off spot," I say. "She'll never get them to the drop-off spot."

She gets them to the drop-off spot. The claw sways, but holds tight.

"Oh, no," Mrs. Webber murmurs.

"Come on," Hannah says. She's up and dashing toward Lexie. Chase and Taylor follow. The claw

opens its metal fingers *and both dolphins drop straight into the chute.*

"Yes!" Lexie cries. I can hear her from the eating area. She tugs the dolphins out of the bin and does a victory dance. "Oh, yea-ah! Oh, yea-ah!"

My mouth hangs open. Something twists in my gut, like a snake. An ugly snake. A jealous snake.

"Oh, that's just fantastic," Mrs. Webber says, I think just to herself. "Nobody ever gets the toy. *N*obody."

The other kids in our class are hurrying over to Lexie.

"So much for natural consequences," Mrs. Webber says. She glances at me. "I suppose it's time to do some damage control, huh, Ty?"

I shrug. I don't know what she means, and the snake inside of me is a mean snake, and anyway, Lexie won *two dolphins*. That's not damage. Plus, it's too late to control, because it already happened.

"You coming?" Mrs. Webber asks.

It's the same question Lexie asked.

"No thanks," I say. I sound like a robot. I feel like a robot. I feel like I'm not me.

When Mrs. Webber heads to the gift shop, I turn and walk the opposite way.

CHAPTER EIGHT

With my backpack over my shoulder, I walk past the beluga whale tank. I know I'm not supposed to go off on my own, but Lexie wasn't supposed to go to the gift shop, either. But she did, and she won two dolphins. Even so, I'll get back before anyone notices.

If anyone even does notice.

A sign by one exhibit says that there are over eight million gallons of water within the aquarium. That's a lot of water. The sign also says that if I look for a really long time into this particular tank, I might see a manta ray named Nandi. NANDI IS THE ONLY MANTA RAY IN A U.S. AQUARIUM, the sign says.

I search for Nandi. Lexie didn't see Nandi,

because Mrs. Hammerdorfer didn't take us this way. Maybe none of the other groups came here, either. Maybe I'll be the only kid in the class to see Nandi. Seeing Nandi would be better than winning two dumb dolphins.

Except Nandi doesn't show up. I peer into the tank until my head hurts, and then I decide I don't even like Nandi.

I leave and look at some eels. They have no eyeballs. The jellyfish don't, either. But they're pretty, how they blob about.

I should go back to my group. Only the mean snake that was twisting in my stomach has turned into a gray day snake. Gray day snakes don't like happy kids who brag about winning dolphins. Gray day snakes like to be alone.

Or maybe they like . . . to be with penguins? Because when I see a sign that says PENGUINS, the snake in my stomach starts to feel less snaky.

I'll visit the penguins, and *then* I'll go back to the group.

I follow the arrow that means "This way for the penguins!" It takes me to a tank, but the tank is empty, and in front of it is another sign. This one says, PENGUINS ARE CURRENTLY NOT IN THE EXHIBITION TANK DUE TO CONSTRUCTION. WE APOLOGIZE FOR THE INCONVENIENCE. HOWEVER, YOU CAN SEE THE PENGUINS UP CLOSE AND PERSONAL ON ONE OF OUR "BEHIND THE SCENES" TOURS. TICKETS ON SALE NOW!

The penguins aren't in the tank? People have to buy tickets to see them? What a rip-off! Plus it says "tickets on sale now," but *where* are they on sale?

I glance around. I don't see anyone, but I do see poles with velvety ropes between them, the kind for when people line up for things. Where the front of the line would be, there's a door. I go over to it.

"Hello?" I say.

No one answers.

I put my hand on the door handle. I just put it there, that's all. Except my hand decides to turn the handle . . . and the door opens.

So I go in. If they didn't want me to, they should have locked it.

At first it's just another exhibit hall, just darker and with no windows showing the outside world. Also, with no other people walking through it. Just me. On both sides of the hall there's stuff to look at, like coral reefs and shark jaws.

I reach a metal staircase. I go up it. When I get to the top, I stop breathing.

I'm *above* the beluga whale tank. I can look down into it, and I can see the beluga whales! They're in the bottommost corner of the tank. That's why we couldn't see them before. But I can see them now, and they glow, they're so white. And lumpy! And really weird-looking and not at all what you think of when you think of the word "whale."

"Hi, beluga whales!" I say quietly, waving at them. My heart is happier now.

Then I spot something that makes my heart *super* happy. The penguins!

I cross the whale-viewing platform and go down a second set of stairs. *And right in front of me is a pen full of penguins!* They're so cute! There are four of them. A mommy and three babies, I think. They have water to play in, and a squeaky toy shaped like a dog bone.

I lean over the wall of the pen, and it's not very high, this wall. I mean, it's too high for a penguin to climb over, but not for a person. Probably the aquarium workers go in and do stuff, like clean up the penguin poop and give them fresh water. Probably they play with them, too. If I was inside a pen of penguins, I'd play with them.

I look from side to side. I'm the only human in here.

One of the babies waddles over to me. His

head is black, and so are the tips of his wings. His tummy is white. He is *not* like an eel or a jellyfish, because he does have eyeballs, and they're dark and shiny and gazing right at me.

"*Piu!*" he says.

I'm ninety-nine percent sure he's saying *hi*, so I say hi back.

He cocks his head and says, "*Piu piu?*"

This time he's asking if I have any fish. I just know it, maybe because I'm secretly part penguin.

I don't have any fish, since Mom didn't pack me any. Is there something else I could give him?

"Hold on," I say. I wiggle my backpack off my shoulder and get out what's left of my peanut butter and jelly sandwich. I wish it was a peanut butter and jelly*fish* sandwich, but oh well. I rip off a piece, then stop. Is peanut butter poisonous to penguins? I don't think so. Jelly? How could jelly be poisonous? Bread? Nothing wrong with bread.

So, okay. I toss the bite of sandwich to my friend Pingy,

which is what I've named this shiny-eyed penguin baby. He scoops it up with his orange beak and jerks his head as he swallows. He flaps his wings. *"Piu? Piu?"*

"Hold your horses, Pingy," I say as I tear off another bite. "It's coming." I toss it into the pen, and Pingy gobbles it up. He's so cute, and his brother and sister aren't playing with him, and his mom is doing something boring to her feathers. None of them is paying attention to Pingy AT ALL.

I think Pingy must have gotten some peanut butter stuck to the roof of his beak, because he goes *mlump-mlump* and stretches his face out, kind of. That happens to me, too! I get peanut butter stuck to the roof of my mouth and make *mlump* sounds, too! But I think this is Pingy's first time, because his eyes get big and he waddles from side to side.

"Piumplf?" he says.

Wow, I think. Wow and wow and wow, because the part of me that understands penguin language knows exactly what Pingy is saying: He wants me to take him home. He also wants to get the peanut butter unstuck, but mainly he wants me to take him home. The other penguins don't care about him, and the aquarium people don't either, probably. Who cares about one little penguin when there are eight million gallons of water full of eels and jellies and beluga whales?

And if the beluga whales can hide, then Pingy can hide, too. He doesn't have to be out in the open *all* the time—especially since the exhibit's closed off, anyway. He could hide in my backpack, which is the exact right size for him. It would be cozy.

I know. I'll lean over the railing and dangle my hand out. If Pingy comes over, that means he's saying, *Yes, please.* If he doesn't, then he doesn't.

There might be a voice in my head saying things I don't like. A voice like Mom's, kind of, saying, "Don't you do it, Ty-bug." But I pretend not to hear it.

I lean over the railing and reach out my hand. I'm breathing faster than normal.

"*Piu?*" Pingy says.

I hold still, even though the railing is digging into my ribs.

Pingy waddles toward me. "*Piu?*"

Maybe my fingers smell like peanut butter, because Pingy juts out his beak and nibbles them. *Wham wham wham* goes my heart, because he's saying, *Yes, please!* He is!

I scoop Pingy up, and he doesn't squirm. He snuggles up close and tries to wedge his beak up under my armpit.

"No, silly," I say, because I need to get him into my backpack.

"*Piu?*" he says as I push him in.

"You have to be quiet, 'kay?" I zip up the backpack, but leave a crack for air. Also so that he can see me and not be scared.

I'm scared, but I try not to be. And plus my whole body is tingling with excitement. I go through the door that says EXIT, and I'm back in the bright and crowded aquarium. I fast-walk toward the food court, careful not to jostle Pingy.

"Ty Perry?" a deep voice says.

I jump. In front of me stands a guard. He's tall and has huge shoulders, and he's wearing a uniform. *And* he's got a walkie-talkie.

"Are you Tyler Perry?"

I start to nod, then stop. Because he's freaky.

"Oh, thank God," Mrs. Webber says, rushing over. "Ty, where have you been?!"

The guard raises his walkie-talkie. "Found the kid," he says into it. "Over."

From the mike comes a crackly response: "Safe and sound? Over."

The guard looks down at me.

I really hope Pingy keeps quiet.

"Yeah, he's fine," the guard says into the walkie-talkie. To me, he says, "Kid, listen. You can't go off like that."

I nod. I nod *a lot*.

"Omigosh, thank you. I'm so sorry for the trouble," Mrs. Webber tells the guard.

"Gotta teach kids to follow the rules," the guard says.

"Thank you, sir," Mrs. Webber says again. In a different voice altogether, she says, "Come on, Ty. Field trip's over."

She's mad. I've never seen her this mad before. Well, except at Taylor sometimes.

But she's never been mad at me.

I try to explain. "I . . . I just . . ."

She grabs my arm and pulls me toward the rest of the class. "I don't want to hear it. I'm *extremely* disappointed in you."

I dig my fingernail into my thumb and press hard. This is the worst field trip ever.

Well, except for Pingy.

But Mrs. Webber would be even madder if she knew Pingy was in my backpack.

So do I tell her?

I don't want to. But if I don't, won't she be even madder-er when she finds out? If she finds out?

Except Mrs. Webber is pretty good at finding things out. When someone does something bad, Mrs. Webber pretty much *always* finds out.

When we reach the rest of my class, everyone stares at me, like, *Ooo, you're in trouble.*

"Um, Mrs. Webber?" I say.

She cuts me off. "No. I'm going to call your mom. *She* can deal with you."

"But—"

"Get with your group. We're leaving."

I go to Lexie and Breezie and Mrs. Hammerdorfer. I use my brain power to tell Pingy to not wiggle or say *piu.*

"Want to see my dolphins?" Lexie asks. "I won

two of them!" She thrusts the fuzzy blue one at me. "You can touch it if you want."

I frown. Lexie broke the rules, and she won two stuffed dolphins.

I broke the rules, and I got yelled at by a guard and Mrs. Webber.

"Touch it!" Lexie commands, wiggling the stuffed dolphin in my face.

I touch it. It feels nothing like a real live sea creature.

CHAPTER NINE

On the drive back, Pingy fills up Mrs. Hammerdorfer's car with a fishy smell. In the aquarium, I didn't realize Pingy had a smell. In Mrs. Hammerdorfer's car with its rolled-up windows, I realize he does.

"Ew," Lexie says. "What's that stink?"

"It's Ty," Breezie says. "Ty, you stink."

I hold my backpack tight. "I've given up baths," I say. "I'm going for the Olympic world record."

Lexie laughs. "Gross."

Mrs. Hammerdorfer makes a disapproving sound.

We arrive at school just in time for pickup. Mom is waiting in her station wagon—not Sandra, but Mom—and I'm so glad to see her. So so so *so* glad, even though she's not going to be happy when she learns about Pingy. I'm even glad to see Teensy Baby Maggie in her car seat.

"Mom?" I say as I climb into the backseat. I'm still not allowed to sit in the front. It's a law. "There's something I—"

"Ty, *hush*," she says. "Do you know why I had to come pick you up today? Do you know why I had to wake Maggie up from her nap so that I could drive out here to get you?"

"Um, but—"

"Not. A. *Word*," Mom says. Her fingers are tight on the steering wheel. "I can't believe you would run off from your class like that! What were you thinking?"

She said *not a word*. Does she want a word now? Or will it make her yell more?

"You could have gotten lost, or kidnapped . . ." Her air comes out in a big burst. "Mrs. Webber had to call *security*! She had to call security to look for *you*!"

"But I wasn't lost *or* kidnapped."

"You could have been."

"But I wasn't."

She glares at me in the rearview mirror. *"Not another word.* And when we get home, you're going straight to your room, and you'll be staying there all night."

Her nose twitches.

"No, strike that. You're going straight upstairs to take a bath, because you smell awful. Why in the world do you smell so awful?"

"Well, that's what—"

"Never mind. Home. Bath. Bed. Do you understand?"

"But Mom, I really need to—"

"No," she snaps.

Teensy Baby Maggie starts crying. Pingy starts *piu*-ing. Mom is scaring all of us.

At least Teensy Baby Maggie's wails cover up Pingy's noises.

I let Teensy Baby Maggie hold my finger. She doesn't let go.

"Shhh," I whisper to both of them. I say it again. "*Shhhhh.*" It sounds a little like a wave sounds when it rolls in at the ocean.

In the bathroom, I close the door and unzip my backpack.

"Come on out, little guy," I say to Pingy. There's a tremble in my voice, and it surprises me. I wedge my hands around his feathered body. Except not exactly feathered. More like . . . fuzzy.

But he's warm, and he doesn't seem banged up, and I am so glad about this that my muscles go loose.

"*Piu?*" he says.

I laugh, although the tremble is still there. But Pingy isn't worried. He's as cute and happy as ever. He twists his head from side to side, like, *So this is where I live now? Cool. Do you have any more peanut butter?*

I set him on the fluffy yellow bathmat.

He pees, making a dark spot.

"Ack! No! You have to pee in the toilet, okay?" I lift him up to show him, but I realize that he's too small. He would fit all the way in, and what if he got flushed?

Bathtub, I think. He can pee in the bathtub, and even though he's already peed, I put him in there anyway. I let go of him, and he takes two slippery steps. Then he squirts out a green squishy poop.

"*Ew,*" I say, giggling. "Pingy!" I wipe it up with toilet paper and flush it down. I soak up the pee stain as best I can and flush it down, too. Then I settle onto my knees and prop my arms on the rim of the tub. Pingy waddles and slips and flaps his wings.

I love him so much. But I'm worried about him, too. About him being here. I don't think a penguin can live in a bathtub forever. And what do penguins eat besides peanut butter?

Fish.

Where do I get fish?

"Piu?" Pingy says. "Piu, piu?"

"Ty!" Mom yells. It sounds like she's at the bottom of the staircase. "I don't hear the water running!"

I stay quiet. I put my finger to my lips to tell Pingy to be quiet, too.

"Winnie, would you go make Ty take his bath?" I hear Mom say.

"Mo-o-m," Winnie calls from her room. "He's seven years old. He can take a bath by himself."

Of course I can, I want to tell them. *BUT NOT WITH A BABY PENGUIN IN THE TUB!*

"Winnie, please. I really can't deal with him right now."

A hole opens up inside me. I rock from my knees onto my bottom. I pull my legs to my chest and wrap my arms around them.

She's mad because she thinks I acted like a baby on purpose, like by running away at the aquarium. Like not taking my bath. But she gets mad when I don't act like a baby, too. Like when I do things all by myself, like get my pacifiers down.

She is being a Big Fat Meanie Mommy. I hug my shins tighter and bury my head between knees.

There are footsteps in the hall, followed by a quick rap on the bathroom door.

I unpretzel my body.

"One sec!" I cry. But before I can hide Pingy—

in a towel? in the cabinet beneath the sink?—
Winnie strides in.

"Ty," she starts, "you've got to take your—" Her
words trickle off. With super-wide eyes, she takes
in Pingy. Pingy takes Winnie in, too.

Winnie turns to me. I try to make my face look
sweet and innocent.

"You have a penguin," she states.

I smile hopefully.

"There is a *penguin* in our bathtub."

"His name is Pingy."

She presses her hands to her eyes, then
drops them. "Holy pickles, Ty." She kneels by
the tub.

"Isn't he so cute?" I ask. "Did I tell you his
name is Pingy?"

"Pingy?"

"You should say hi to him," I say. It's better
having Winnie in here with me. I didn't think it
would be, but it is. It makes me excited again.

"Um, hi, Pingy," Winnie says. She glances at me. "Wait—how do you know he's a he?"

"I just do?"

Winnie reaches her hand out, then draws it back. "Can I . . . touch him?"

"Sure. Just be gentle."

Winnie strokes Pingy's head. He nudges up against her palm.

"*Piu. Piu piu,*" he says.

"Awww," Winnie says. "He likes me!"

"He might be hungry." I pause. "He likes peanut butter."

Winnie grins. Then all at once she pulls her hand away and wipes off her grin.

"So you stole this baby penguin from the aquarium?" she demands.

"I didn't mean to."

"You can't steal penguins. You can't steal, period." She looks at me. "You know that, Ty."

I hunch my shoulders.

"Don't you think his mom is missing him?"
Winnie asks.

"She wasn't even paying attention to him. She
was just picking at her feathers."

"That doesn't mean she won't miss her baby
when she realizes he's gone."

"*Piu piu,*" Pingy says.

I hold very still. There's something about his
pius that sounds . . . different.

"He doesn't sound happy," Winnie says.

"Yes he does," I say. But he doesn't. This is
the first time his *pius* have sounded the opposite
of happy. Unhappy. For some reason, I think of
Price, and also of Price's mom, walking out of
Trinity after dropping him off.

"What's wrong, Pingy?" I say.

"Maybe you're right and he's hungry," Winnie
says. "You say he likes peanut butter?"

"Uh-huh."

She gets to her feet. "I'll go get it so Mom

doesn't see you out of the tub. And you should ... *ack*. Can Pingy swim?"

"I don't know. Probably?"

She pulls her hair off her neck, holds it there for a second, then lets it fall back over her shoulders. She does that when she's thinking.

"Okay," she says. "I'll go get the peanut butter. You hold Pingy in your lap—not in the tub—and turn on the bathwater so that Mom doesn't come barging in. You don't want her to come barging in, believe me."

"Then what?"

"Don't know. We'll figure it out."

"But what if he poops on me?"

"Then you'll have penguin poop on you." Her hand's on the doorknob, but she hasn't yet opened the door. "I can't believe you stole a penguin from the Georgia Aquarium."

"It has over eight million gallons of water," I offer.

"And you're telling me that because . . . ?"

"Because that's a lot of water. With a lot of sea creatures in it." I bite my lip. "So maybe they won't miss one teeny-tiny penguin?"

"Believe me, they will," Winnie says.

Strangely, that makes me feel better.

CHAPTER TEN

Winnie comes back with peanut butter *and* our older sister, Sandra.

"Here's the thing," Sandra says, after a lot of finger-drumming on her jeans.

"Yes?" Winnie says.

I look up at the two of them and wait.

The tub is full of water.

I'm sitting cross-legged on the bathroom floor, and Pingy is in my lap. Each time he says *"piu,"* I give him a lick of peanut butter. Each time he finishes, he says *"piu"* again. He's saying *"piu"* a lot. I think he misses his mom. I feel REALLY bad.

But I'm glad Sandra and Winnie are here. Together, we'll figure something out.

Sandra collects air in her cheeks, then blows

it out. "Okay. Mom is stressed. The last thing she needs is to find out she's harboring a stolen penguin."

She zeroes in on me. "Ty, you've learned your lesson, right? That you shouldn't steal a baby penguin ever ever again?"

"He has," Winnie says.

"I have," I say. "I have totally learned that lesson. I *promise.*"

"Hmmph," Sandra says.

"I think you're suggesting that there's no reason to bring Mom into it—or Dad—and personally, I agree," Winnie says.

"I do, too!" I say.

Sandra puts her hands on her hips. "Yeah, but how are we going to get Pingy back to the aquarium without bringing Mom into it?"

"We just will," Winnie says. "You can drive us there. We'll say we're going on an errand. And then . . . um . . . you'll use your feminine wiles to hand Pingy over to someone who works there."

"Why do I have to use *my* feminine wiles?" Sandra says. "Why can't you use yours?"

"I will. That's why I'm coming, too," Winnie says.

I don't know what feminine wiles are, but I do know that my big sisters can pretty much do anything they set their minds to.

"Do I have boy wiles?" I ask. "Should I use them when we get to the aquarium?"

"No, because you're staying here," Sandra says.

"But—"

"You have to take your bath," Winnie says. "Plus, you're already in enough trouble. No way will Mom let us take you out of the house."

I pout, but not for long. I cuddle Pingy close and say, "You're going home! Hurray!"

"*Piu-piu!*" he says in lonely *piu-piu* language.

"Ack." Sandra groans. "Does he have to keep making that sound? How can we sneak him out of here when he's being so loud? He only shuts up when he's got peanut butter in his mouth, and we can't keep giving him peanut butter all the way out to the car."

"It would look weird if I keep dipping my hand into my messenger bag or whatever," Winnie says. "Mom would ask questions."

"We could put the container of peanut butter in there with him," Sandra says. "Except, no, because he'd flop around trying to get to it, and flap his wings and stuff, and . . . *no*."

"Oh, Pingy," Winnie says. "Can't you just stay quiet?"

"*Piu*," Pingy says, and with his dark eyes he looks at me.

Not Sandra.

Not Winnie.

Me.

A lump rises in my throat. I have to fix this. I *have* to come up with an idea. I scrunch my forehead and push hard with my brain muscles—and I do!

"I know what to do!" I say, doing my standing-up-without-my-hands trick and passing Pingy to Winnie. "Here, hold Pingy. I'll be right back."

I dart to my bedroom. I feel around on my sheets. Yes!

I dash back to the bathroom and wave ol' greenie proudly.

"Your old pacifier?" Sandra says.

"Yep." I dip it into the peanut butter and pull up a big blob. "This'll last for a *long* time. And if he's got peanut butter in his mouth, he'll be quiet in Winnie's backpack. See?"

Winnie and Sandra look at each other.

"Watch," I say. I stick greenie into Pingy's beak, and right away he goes *suck-suck-suck*. He stops fidgeting in Winnie's arms, too.

"Brilliant!" Winnie says. She kisses me. "Ty? You are brilliant."

I grin.

Sandra pushes herself off the sink. "Right. We better go, then."

I pet Pingy's head. "Bye, Pingy. You're a good Pingy."

He keeps sucking greenie. He looks so cute, sucking a real live pacifier.

"You can visit him next time you go to the aquarium," Winnie says. She tucks Pingy under the bottom of her shirt so that she can sneak him to her room, where her messenger bag is. Mom's downstairs, but just in case.

"Don't forget me, 'kay?" I tell Pingy.

"Take your bath, squirt," Sandra says. "We'll keep Pingy safe."

They leave, and for a long time I stare at the ceiling, thinking of things that could go wrong. But for every wrong thing, there's a way they could make it right.

Like, if the aquarium is closed, they'll find a security guard.

If the security guard gets suspicious, Sandra will make up a good story. Or Winnie will, because she's awesome at stories, and Sandra will look wise and responsible like someone who'll be going to college next year.

And if Pingy doesn't want to go back to his aquarium pen . . .

Well, he will, because that's where he lives. And his exhibit won't be under construction forever. When Mom isn't so mad, I'll see if she'll take me to the aquarium just for fun, and Teensy Baby Maggie can come, too. I won't mention Pingy. I'll just say how much Maggie will love it there.

I'm pretending I'm a jellyfish when Mom knocks on the door. "Ty?" she says. "Can I come in?"

"Um . . . I guess," I say.

I sit up and squeeze my legs together for privacy reasons. Water sloshes over the edge of the tub.

She steps into the bathroom with Teensy Baby Maggie in one arm and Teensy Baby Maggie's bouncy seat in the other. She puts the bouncy seat on the floor and puts Maggie in it. She closes the lid on the toilet and sits down.

"Sweetie, I'm worried I haven't been paying enough attention to you," Mom says.

I raise my eyebrows. I thought I was going to get yelled at some more.

"It's just that new babies take a lot of work," she goes on.

"So I've heard . . . and heard . . . and *heard*," I say.

She lets out a small laugh, but her eyes are sad. "Is that why you ran away at the aquarium?"

"I didn't run away! I just wandered away. Accidentally."

"I don't want you *wandering* off from your teacher ever again," she says. "When Mrs. Webber told me what happened, I couldn't believe it. That kind of behavior . . . it's just not like you."

"Because it wasn't me. It was a fake me."

"A fake you?"

A *mad* me, that was the real reason. Mad and sad and other things, too. Like everything was wrong inside of me.

Mom's waiting.

"I won't run away from Mrs. Webber again," I promise. "*Or* wander."

Mom looks at me. I look at her.

"Hmm," she finally says. "Well, do you think you need to be punished some more, or do you think you've been punished enough?"

Parents ask dumb questions sometimes.

"I think I've been punished enough," I say. "But, Mom?"

"Yes?"

"You *do* pay too much attention to Teensy Baby Maggie. Not always! And I know, I know, she's a baby."

Maggie burps.

"But maybe you could do things with just me sometimes?"

"I like that idea," Mom says. "Special time, just for us."

"Yeah! Special time just for us. But other times, we can do stuff with Maggie and Dad and Sandra and Winnie, too." Like the aquarium, but I'll mention that another day.

"It's a plan," Mom says. Her tone says the "talk" part of our talk is over. "And now I have a favor to ask you. I'd ask one of your sisters, but they've gone off on some crazy errand. I didn't quite catch what it was."

"Huh," I say. "Well, they're crazy all right."

"Anyway, I need to get dinner on the table. Can you babysit your sister while I finish up in the kitchen?"

Me? I think. *Babysit Maggie?*

"I think she'd really enjoy some time with her big brother."

"Oh," I say. "Um, okay."

She smiles her special Ty smile, which means *Love you, bug.*

Then she leaves. It's just me and Maggie.

I do like her pretty blue eyes.

"Want me to make dolphin sounds?" I ask her. "Or would you rather feel my loose tooth?"

She does her *pluh* sound.

"Here," I say, taking her weensie finger and putting it on my front tooth. It only wiggles a little, but Maggie thinks it's neat. I know because she kicks her chubby legs.

"I'm sorry I called you a Big Fat Meanie Baby," I tell Maggie. I bite my lip. "And now do you want to hear my dolphin impression?"

She kicks her legs *and* waves her arms.

"To do it, I have to go underwater. But I'll be right back up, 'kay?"

I gaze into her eyes so that she'll know she can trust me. Then I slide underwater and scream. The water muffles it just the right amount, and I know Maggie is impressed, because when I burst back into the air, Maggie is *still* looking at me. And maybe . . . maybe I can do more things to

impress her as I get to know her better, and as she gets to know me. Things like catching two dolphins in a claw machine game, only better.

She likes animals, I can tell because she liked my underwater sea creature noise, so—I know! I should get her a pet! Or, I should get me a pet and share it with her! And we could teach it tricks and love it and be nice to it and name it Chepito!

Hmm. I wonder what kind of pet we'll get. I'll have to give that some thought. For now, I go under again, and I learn something awesome. If I hold my lips in a small-sized O instead of scream-sized O, and if I push out a whole series of Baby Maggie's *pluhs*, I sound almost exactly like a baby penguin.

READ THE NEXT BOOK STARRING TY!